JOEY and JET

TO ABBY AND SIMONE,
WHO LOVE A GOOD BOY-AND-DOG STORY

SIMON AND SCHUSTER
First published in Great Britain in 2004 by Simon & Schuster UK Ltd,
Africa House, 64-78 Kingsway, London WC2B 6AH • Originally
published in 2004 by Atheneum Books for Young Readers, an imprint
of Simon & Schuster Children's Publishing Division, New York • Text
and illustrations copyright © 2004 James Yang • The right of James
Yang to be identified as the author and illustrator of this work has been
asserted by him in accordance with the Copyright, Designs and Patents
Act, 1988 • Book designed by Polly Kanevsky • The text for this book is
set in Tarzana • The illustrations are rendered in digital pen and ink •
All rights reserved, including the right of reproduction in whole or in
part in any form • A CIP catalogue record for this book is available from
the British Library upon request • ISBN 0-689-86112-5 • Manufactured
in China • 10 9 8 7 6 5 4 3 2 1

JOEY and JET

James Yang

SIMON AND SCHUSTER
london new york sydney

This is Joey.

This is the ball.

This is Jet.

"Fetch!"

Jet chases the ball

among
the birds . . .

through the trees . . .

on

the water . . .

down
the
hill . . .

up

the

hill . . .

across the street . . .

between
the
tables . . .

over the roofs . . .

into
a
hole and . . .

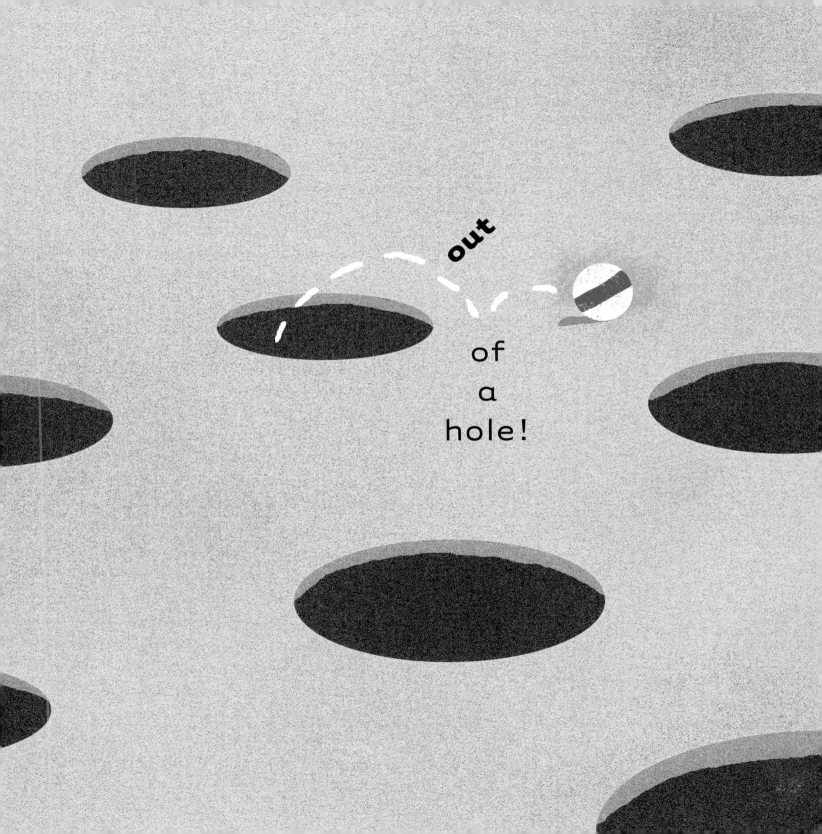

out
of
a
hole!

Jet found his ball and ran . . .

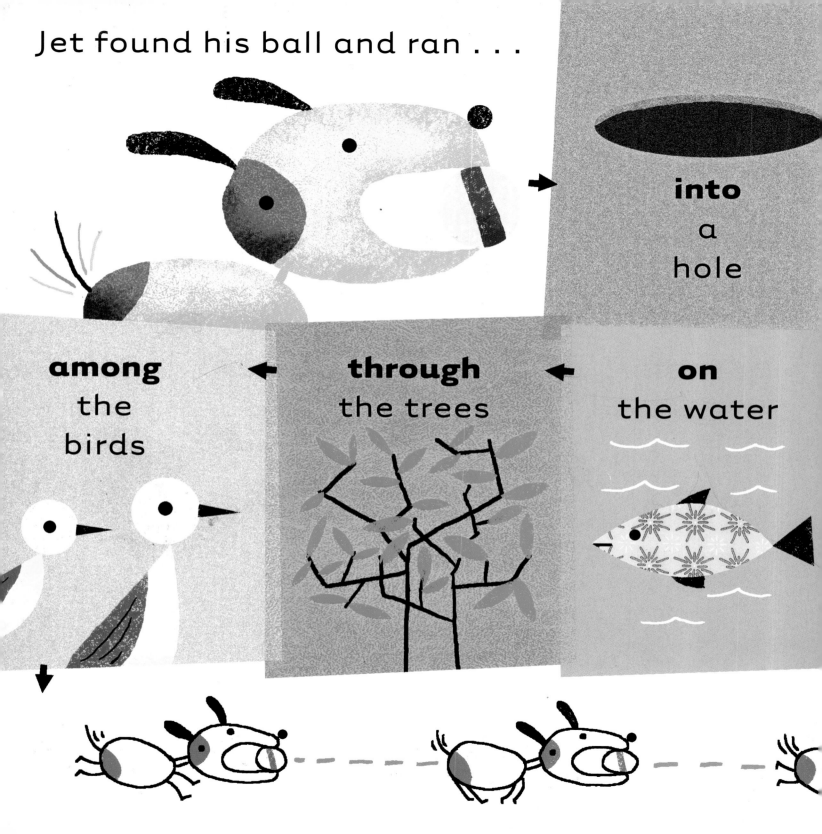

into
a
hole

on
the water

through
the trees

among
the
birds

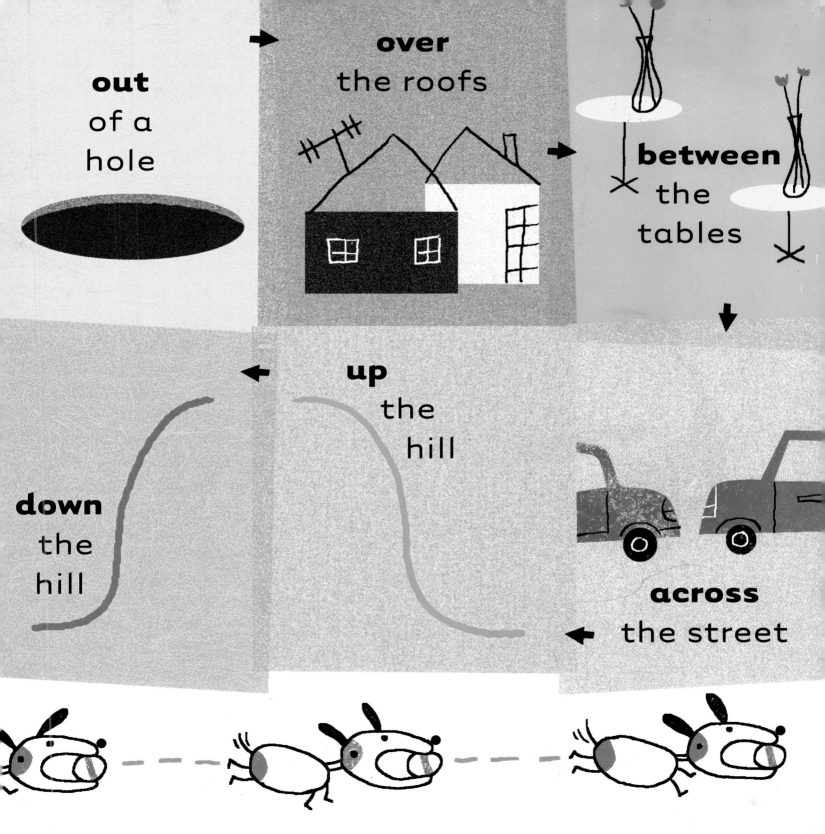

and back
to
Joey!

"Good boy!" said Joey.

Jet is the best ball chaser in the world.

A dog's work is never done.